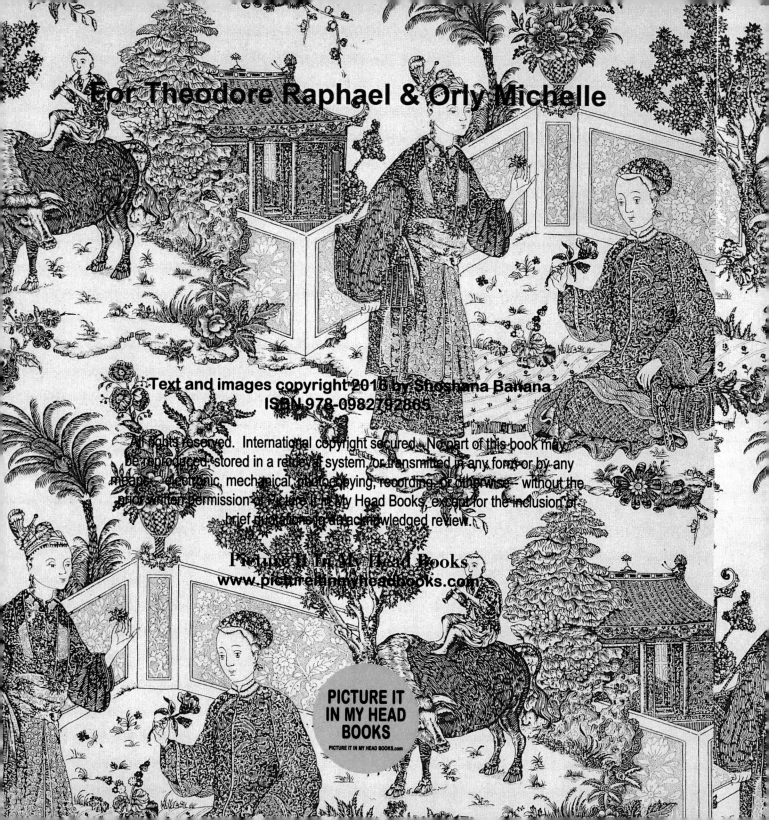

For Theodore Raphael & Orly Michelle

Text and images copyright 2016 by Shoshana Banana
ISBN 978-0982792865

Picture It In My Head Books
www.pictureitinmyheadbooks.com

PICTURE IT
IN MY HEAD
BOOKS

PICTURE IT IN MY HEAD BOOKS.com

LEVI & AYA

(a semi-fictional multi-culti love story)

by Shoshana Banana

When gold was discovered there in 1849, crowds of people rushed to California to make their fortunes.   Among them was a young Jewish man from Germany named Loeb Strauss.

His nickname was **LEVI**.
He worked together with his sisters and brothers, selling clothing and fabric.

Calico is a printed cotton fabric named after Calcutta, India, where it was first made.

In those days,
the safest way to get
from the Strauss Brothers'
shop in New York City
to San Francisco was by
sailing all the way
around South America.
The journey took six
months.
During that time, LEVI
prayed and thought
about the kind of person
he wanted to be in America.
He wanted to be a
good man, who never let
the opportunity of a
mitzvah sail by him.

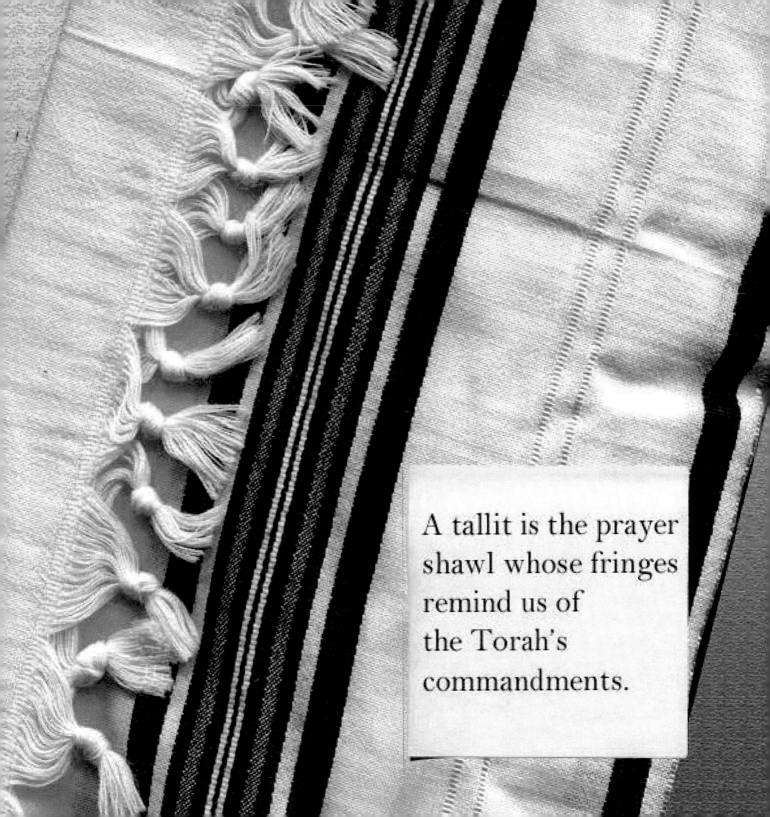

A tallit is the prayer shawl whose fringes remind us of the Torah's commandments.

San Francisco was a wonder.
The bay sparkled blue,
the thick fog descended
like curtains of spun silver,
and people from all corners
of the world pursued their dreams.

Toile (pronounced "twal") is the French word for cloth and is used to describe fabric printed with scenes like this.

The fortune cookie,
widely thought to be
of Chinese origin,
was first introduced
to 19th century
San Franciscans
by a Japanese tea lover.

One sunny day, Levi was downtown,
attending to some business,
when he met a clever silk merchant
named AYA.
She was from Japan, and like Levi,
was running the San Francisco office
of her family business.
Over a cup of tea that tasted to Levi
like grass misted with perfume,
Aya told him that her name is common among
fabric families because it means
"colored design" in Japanese.
"That's funny," Levi said,
"In Hebrew, it means 'a swiftly flying bird'
and is also a great name for a girl."
They became best friends.

Their teas together were always
a pleasure. Every Friday,
LEVI sent a fresh challah from
his sister's oven to Aya's store.
In thanks,
AYA always sent an ever more
beautiful handkerchief.

Japanese indigo, called Ai (pronounced "I") produces a brilliant shade of blue that was widely known as "Japan Blue" in Levi's time.

One drizzly day,
the postman brought Levi
a letter from the next door
state of Nevada.
It was from a Jewish tailor
named JACOB DAVIS:

The US Post transported letters by railroad in those days.

Levi Strauss & Co.
14-16 Battery Street
San Francisco, CA

DATE July .2, 1872

Dear Mr. Levi Strauss,
I say with all humbleness that
I have invented the best pants
in the world.
My secret: metal rivets on the
weak spots that usually rip.
I am selling so many in this here
small town that I can't keep up
with all the orders!
How about you and me become partners
and make more of these pants together
in your fancy-schmancy San Francisco
factory?

Yours sincerely,
Jacob Davis

Over a pot of tea,
LEVI showed the letter to AYA,
soliciting her opinion of it.
"Personally speaking,"
she replied,
"I'd prefer a silk gown any day,
but as a businessperson,
I think this new idea will prove
to be a gold mine."

The pine tree is called "matsu" in Japanese. "Matsu" also means "to wait", so pine has a romantic feeling.

This is a painted copy of a woodblock print from the 1830's by the Japanese artist Hokusai.

LEVI began making the pants.
They sold like hotcakes,
and by and by,
LEVI became a wealthy man.
Looking out over the vast Pacific Ocean
from his balcony,
he would watch the sea traffic,
and reflect on the person
he'd always wanted to be.

See how different money looked in the 19th century?

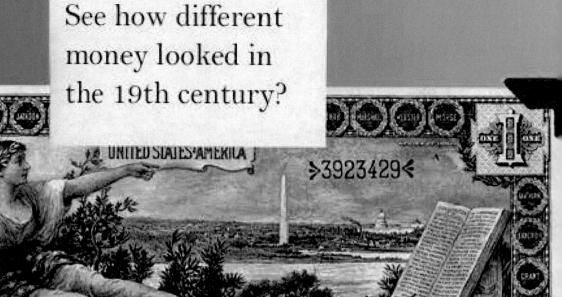

AYA, too, strove to be a good person.
She told LEVI about her cultivation of
"itawari no kokoro",
which means in Japanese
"loving kindness heart."
"That's funny," LEVI said,
"In Hebrew, we call that
'gemilut chasadim',
the gift of loving kindness,
and that's what's behind my plan."
He told her about his dream
to spend as much money as he
could helping others.

LEVI's money helped build
San Francisco's first synagogue,
as well as orphanages,
elderly homes,
and schools.
He became widely known
as a philanthropist who never missed
a major mitzvah opportunity.

A tallit is often stored in a beautiful blue velvet bag like this one.

The hydrangea
blossom comes
from Asia
and was first seen
by Europeans
in the 19th century.

When AYA married a distant relative
from her hometown,
LEVI made her a wedding kimono
out of denim,
and a three-piece suit for her groom,
whose family name was Ido,
after their village.
"That's funny," declared LEVI,
"Ido is a Hebrew name, too.
It means mighty.
And it sure will take
an extraordinary man to be worthy
of you."

LEVI STRAUSS never married nor had children,
but the popularity of his blue jeans
spread around the whole world.
They came to symbolize everything good
about America, especially the freedom,
goodwill, and generosity of spirit
found in friendships
like the one between

AYA IDO and **LEVI STRAUSS**.

Even today,
the favorite jean in Japan
is the one made by
Levi Strauss & Company, USA.

THE DENIM BIBLE

Lightning 特別編集

ザ・デニムバイブル

for tasty life
エイムック2533

デニムの教科書

100年以上も基本的なデザイン
を変えず、もはや身を包むだけ
でなく、ライフスタイルの一部と
なっている稀有な衣類、それが
デニムパンツ。その誕生から現
代までの歴史、価値あるヴィン
テージの変遷、発展を共にした
ユースカルチャー、最新デニム
ブランドカタログ……。基礎から
専門知識まで、デニムのすべて
を網羅したのが、本書である。

A real page from a
popular magazine
published in
Kyoto, Japan.

Author's note

As a fashion historian, I've long been interested in the
blue jean. It is arguably the most beloved and iconic
American artifact sold the world over, synonymous with
integrity, style, attractiveness, youth, and
durability. It is as American as apple pie and the Fourth
of July. Many people, American and international alike,
are unaware that the blue jean was first designed, made,
patented, sold, and publicized by two Jewish immigrants,
Levi Strauss and Jacob Davis. Hailing respectively from
Germany and Lithuania, the founding fathers of the denim
fashion tradition came to the Wild West to escape anti-
Semitic persecution and to test their faith in the American
Dream. Their bravery and confidence informed, from the
very beginning, the blue jean's image as the garment of
choice for adventurers, artists, and dreamers. That legacy
of Jewish-American pioneers lives on in the jeans we wear
today.

In researching this history, I came to appreciate, again
and again, the contribution of the Asian immigrants who
came to San Francisco at the same time as Strauss and
Jacob. I then took fictional license to imagine Levi
Strauss' reaction to the city in which he lived and
thrived.

I do hope you'll indulge my fantasizing long enough to dive
into the multi-culti Jewish world of the American Wild
West.

Shoshana Banana

Shoshana Banana, also known as Hillary Bennahum, loves cotton candy, trampolines, temporary tattoos, blue herons, birch forests, crystals, chrysanthemums, the Dead Sea, castle hotels, express trains, leather books, ginger hot chocolate, animal topiary, and silly monograms.

Made in the USA
Middletown, DE
21 February 2016